MUMMY NEVER TOLD ME

Babette Cole

A Tom Maschler Book
JONATHAN CAPE
LONDON

Mummy never told me that life
is full of little secrets.

Like, what is my
tummy button
for . . .

and how did it get there?

Why is Mummy so busy
that she has no time for me?

Why must I go to school . . .

when Mummy was expelled from hers?

What does the tooth fairy

really look like?

QUACK!

Mummy never told me that
boys are different from girls . . .

or that
it's hard
to tell

the grown-up
ones apart!

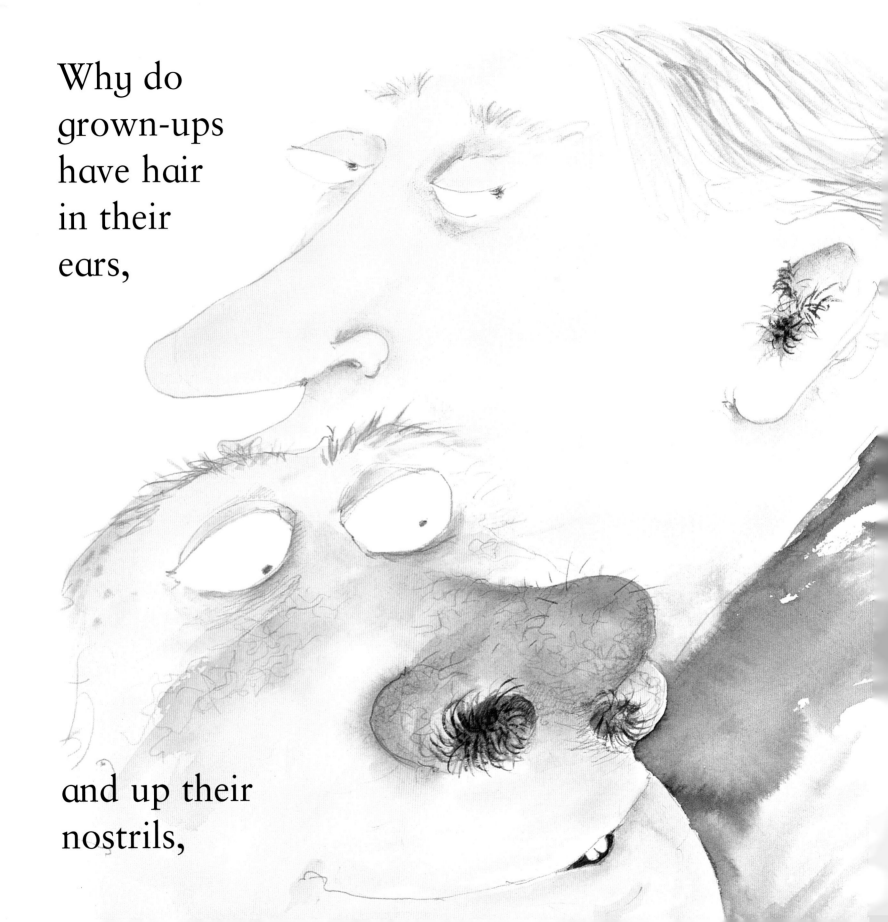

Why do
grown-ups
have hair
in their
ears,

and up their
nostrils,

but sometimes
none on their
heads?

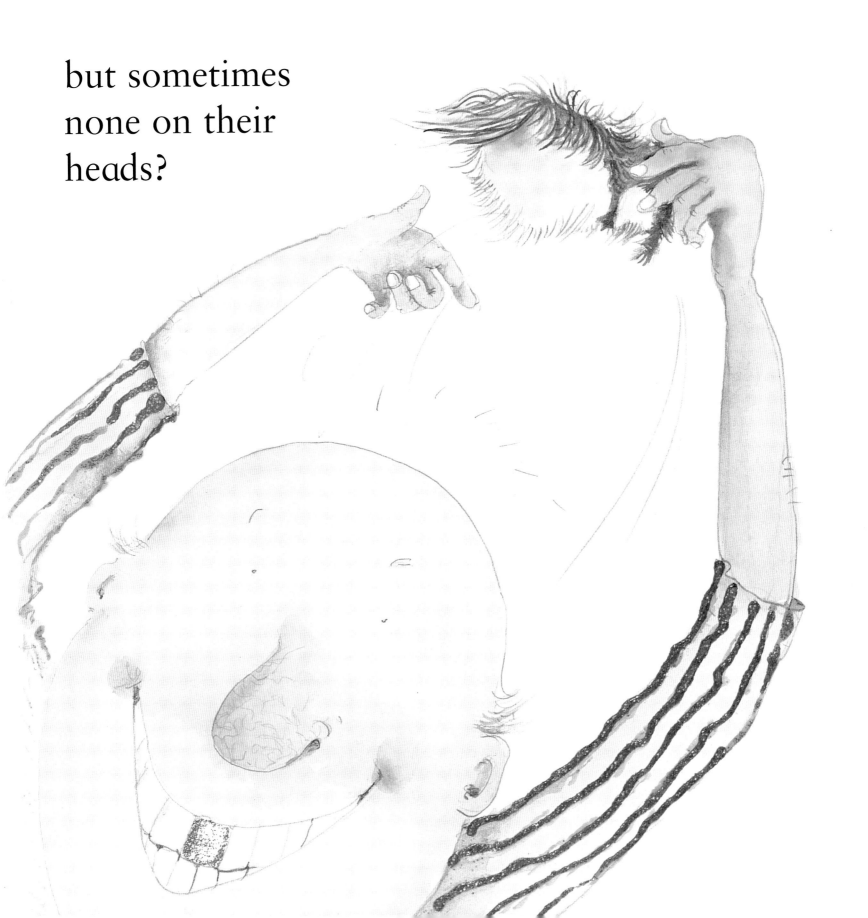

Doctors can help them
choose a new nose.

But they don't tell you what
to do with the old ones!

NOSE PIE

She didn't tell me why
some grown-ups go to sleep
with their teeth in a jar beside them,

or why they
spend so long
in the bathroom!

Why do Mummy and Daddy

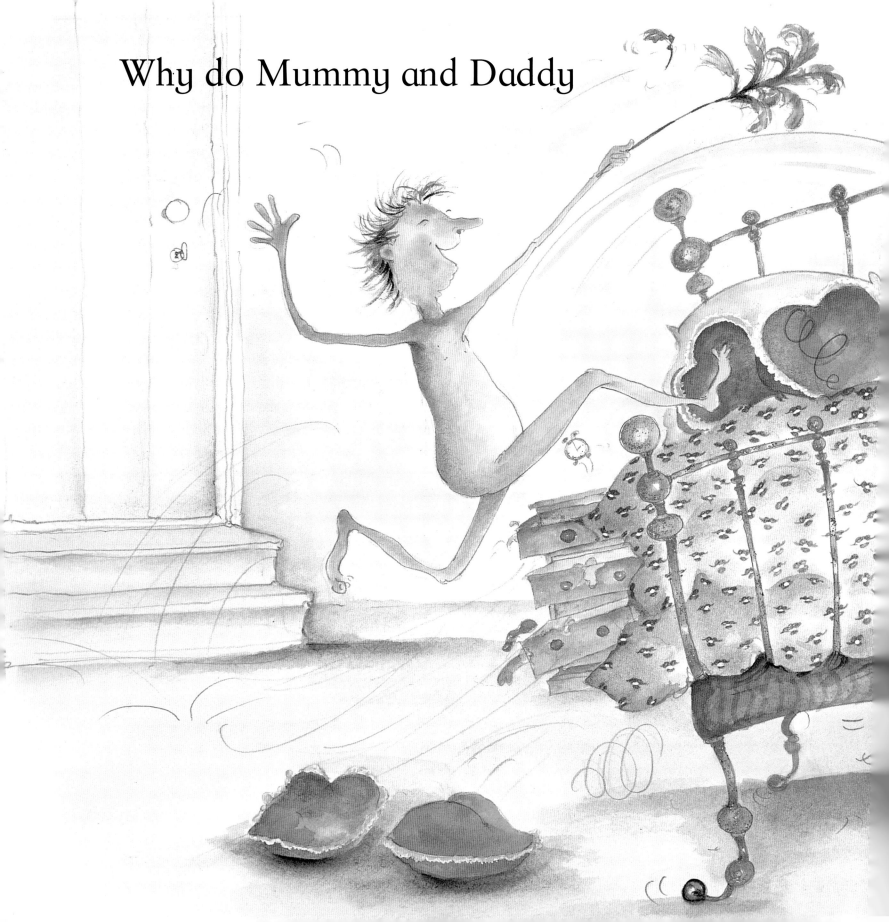

lock me out of their bedroom?

Where do they go

at night?

Where do mummies and daddies
who can't have babies get one from?

How can you
hate someone . . .

and love them
at the same
time?

Why do some women prefer to
fall in love with other women . . .

and some men
with other men?

But I'm not worried.
She'll tell me when the time comes!

To Boo

MUMMY NEVER TOLD ME
A JONATHAN CAPE BOOK: 0 224 04736 1

Published in Great Britain by Jonathan Cape,
an imprint of Random House Children's Books

This edition published 2003

1 3 5 7 9 10 8 6 4 2

RANDOM HOUSE CHILDREN'S BOOKS
61-63 Uxbridge Rd, London W5 5SA
A division of The Random House Group Ltd
RANDOM HOUSE AUSTRALIA (PTY) LTD
20 Alfred Street, Milsons Point, Sydney,
New South Wales 2061, Australia
RANDOM HOUSE NEW ZEALAND LTD
18 Poland Road, Glenfield, Auckland 10, New Zealand
RANDOM HOUSE (PTY) LTD
Endulini, 5A Jubilee Road, Parktown 2193, South Africa

THE RANDOM HOUSE GROUP Limited Reg. No. 954009
www.kidsatrandomhouse.co.uk
www.babette-cole.com

A CIP catalogue record for this book is available from the British Library

Printed in Singapore by Tien Wah Press [PTE] Ltd